One hundred and one rhymes wot I done!

by Angie Shingleton

Contents

4

1: Hidden peas

I'm not a fan of hidden Peas
in noodles and in rice
The texture gives a shock
that I don't think is very nice

Some dishes seem to show off
to see how many there can be
I had Sweet and sour Chicken
and I picked out 53

I don't mind if I can see them
so I know what's coming next
but sneaking in my noodles
doth get me rather vexed

I know there's bigger issues
so do forgive me please
but I had to get it off my chest
I just don't like hidden Peas!

2: If you could sing a Rainbow

If you could sing a Rainbow,
please tell, how would that sound?
Would the sweetest notes in all the world
ring out in what you'd found?

If you could air hug all the world
and spread a song of love
would you then feel satisfied
that you had done enough?

If you could make all dreams come true,
would you save one for yourself
or take comfort that you'd wished
all others happiness and wealth?

Every smile you share each day
helps someone else along their way

Each hello and how are you
could be helping someone through

So sing your Rainbow every day
Air hug the world in your own way
The wish you long to make come true
could simply be a smile from you!

3: Bert, the frog

Once there was a frog called Bert
He liked a little Cider
One night he got so liquored up
He made friends with a spider

His friends, the mice all laughed at him
but Bert said, there's no harm
He's a rather splendid fellow
and he spins a damn good yarn

4: Middleagedness

I thought that I was poorly
Was dizzy when I'd stand
Had a spot upon my chin
and a crinkle on my hand

I'd wake myself by cracking
Joints aren't what they used to be
Thought I needed a new hip,
two elbows and a knee

A double shot of Evening Primrose
and a little stretching too
just made me want a nap
so I guessed it must be flu

Then I googled all my symptoms
and am embarrassed to confess
It seems I simply have a bout
of middleagedness

5: Passport photo

I needed a new passport
I decided that I would
put on a face of makeup
so my photo would look good

I took a billion selfies
My buddy helped out too
but when I looked back through them
I only liked a few

But that's ok I thought
I only need the one
I'll have a gorgeous passport
by the time the uploads done

But no, my pictures failed
the many stringent rules
They seem to want a mugshot
or for us to look like fools

No shadows are allowed
Well how do you suppose
I manage to do that
with this bloomin' pointy nose

No smiling and no frown
Just something in between
Now I'm posing whilst not posing
and I look like a baked bean

Of course the baked bean photo passed
all the regs that make it lawful
and once again my passport
has a photo which is awful

6: Drinks

I met a wee pup one day in the pub
He asked about when I was young
If we didn't have all the drinks they have now
how on earth did we all have such fun

Well, I explained, when I were a girl
we only had one kind of Cider
It wasn't about which fruit it once were
t'was 'bout getting it quickly inside ya

If you liked Beer you'd get more for your
pound
and there was plenty to choose
and when you had finished your sup from the
bottle
you could wear the tops on your shoes

Then times got mad, people branched out
and put Alcohol in Lemonade

and then came the sweetness of 20/20
and some of our best times were made
So, I explained, you sure mustn't fret
we saw it all from the beginning
and how great that we did cos these days my
friend,
too much fruit juice can set me off singing

7: She tiptoed through the brambles

She tiptoed through the brambles
She didn't want to say
that she'd felt a little nervous
would have gone the other way

She stepped across the stream
as it babbled round her calves
She'd rather brave the water
than be the butt of laughs

She ducked beneath the cobweb
and hoped the spider gone
She thought she couldn't do this
but it seemed that she'd been wrong

She paused to thank a friendly bird
that sang her on her way

and smiled up at the sunshine
that had kept the cold at bay
She now skipped through the brambles
as she found another gear
She was stronger than she thought
She'd no longer live in fear

8: Food fight

The bin lid gave an almighty crash as the
daring fox checked out his stash
The cubs were hungry, t'was time for tea.
He'd been as quiet as he could be
Twitching curtains made a light appear, but
he had a task, no time for fear
he kept his head down, continued to poke,
didn't see the approach of the rival he'd woke
People gasped as the soaring kite, swooped
down to the garden with all his might
But not this time, fox leapt and landed, "The
missus will flip if I'm empty handed"
The kite agreed, "You win this time, if your
wife is anything like mine
I can't be responsible for the grief if you go
back with empty teeth"
The fox, relieved, grinned real wide and he
felt all warm and glad inside

He turned around to sort his snack then had
a thought that took him aback
"Why thanks" began the fox with glee. "but
how wonderful this night could be
if I, from the ground and you, from the air,
divide this out and we both share"
Children watched that night and learned that
the greatest gifts are often earned
through kindness and generosity and having
people round for tea

9: I'd like to be your shoe

I'd like to be your shoe
so I'm everywhere you goes
I'd hug you nice and tightly
and play piggies with your toes

10: Take a moment

Take a moment
don't check the time
just have faith
all will fit in fine

Kiss your lover
hug your mate
phone a friend
cos time don't wait

Ssh ssh slow down
hide your list
of things to do
they won't get missed

Take the time
to rest your mind
restore your soul
and mend your bind

Close your eyes
let your mind drift
and take a moment
to enjoy this gift

11: Going dating

I've made big plans you know
not one to sit and cry
won't feel sorry for myself
just because I've lost my guy

I've packed up all my memories
all ready for my move
got new stuff like a spatula
I'm a big girl now, I'll prove

I've bought some flowery plates
to put my awesome cooking on
and I'll go on loads of dates
now that he's upped and gone

I'll travel here and there
have a lifetime of adventures
I'll write another thirty books
before I get my dentures

I'll join a class of exercise
and hey, why not, a choir
I'll live life to the fullest
and I'm never gonna tire

I'll work out every day
and show him what he's missing
He'll think, God damn she's fine
and wonder who I'm kissing

But the bugger is I'm lazy
and my brand new life's still waiting
cos I've got a comfy sofa and
new Celebs go dating!

12: I'm a Dandelion

I'm a Dandelion
and I'm beautiful
I'm yellow
and I'm happy

If you think that
I'm a problem weed
maybe you just
need a nappy

When I'm done
I shed my hue
and then I
really rock

You can blow me
now to tell the time
I'm a most
delightful clock

So smile at me
as you pass by
just as you would
the others

The buttercups
and primroses
My much loved
yellow brothers

Don't write me off
I mean no harm
I think it
such a pity

To be regarded
as a weed
when I too am
super pretty

13: Good intentions

New year, new start

I'll make a plan
on how I'll be
a better woman

I'll get more fit
and lose my belly
read more books
and watch less telly

I'll be astute
make sure I call

my friends before

they even fall

Get my hair cut
more regularly

If my hair's happy
then I shall be

I'll clear my piles
and use a drawer
and see the carpet
like before

It's a mighty plan
I'm a little shaken

I'm heading back

to bed with bacon

14: It is not wrong

It is not wrong
to feel not strong
It shows that
you are feeling

It is not bad
when you are sad
It shows that
you are dealing

Don't be sorry
when you worry
It shows that
you are giving

Don't be wary
when life feels scary
It shows that
you are living

15: Guinness
(at The Mad STad)

I went to see the rugby
A record was in sight
Practise was taking place
every morning, noon and night

On matchday the sun was shining
and the pitch was looking swell
The drums were banging loudly
and we sang real good as well

We lost 4 tries to 2
but we triumphed. How d'ya think?
We battered last year's tally
of how much Guinness we could drink

16: Words have failed me today

Just one rhyme Angie and then you can chill
You can feel you've achieved, then do as you
will

How hard can it be, just write what you're
thinking
Appraise the weather or joke about drinking

Ten minutes later as I stare at the page
it appears my vocabulary's having a rage

I've run out of ideas already it seems
Now i'm wonderin' how people come up with
new memes

Now i'm off on a tangent that really won't
help
and now I can't rhyme here except if I yelp

If you've flicked through this book and are
reading this first
I'm sorry you've come to what might be the
worst

I alone could wibble so much just to say
that I have no words. Words have failed me
today

17: Uncle Herbert's bong

I had an Uncle, let's call him Herbert
He liked a smoke after a sherbet
but it was forbidden, Aunt Mildred said
so he did his smoking in the shed

One day Aunt Mildred caught the smell
and marched down there to give him hell
we saw at once something was wrong
as we all saw Uncle Herbert's bong

"But it is the 60s" we heard him claim
Uncle Herbert was having flashbacks again
She clouted him, he gave a scream
and we all got to have ice-cream

To take his secret to the grave
to tell no stories, to behave
To never speak of what or how
except of course, I've told you now

18: Cutlery Tray

Ponder if you had not a cutlery tray
The spoons with the knives, forks in disarray

You look for a teaspoon when needing to stir
and the whisk poppeth out hoping for a whirr

Spatulas for corkscrews won't open your
drink
Such mess, might as well leave it all in the
sink

And believe me my friend this is only a taster
You can't light the oven with a darn turkey
baster

So whatever else you do with this day
Thank goodness that you have a cutlery tray

19: Baby Girl

I wonder what you're dreaming

as I glance and see you smile

It makes my heart the happiest

it's been in quite a while

I wonder what you're thinking

when you watch me as I sing

Are you thinking we'll be friends

Are you thinking anything

I wonder of your future

as I sit, amazed by you

I pray all your dreams are happy

ones and that they all come true

20: Real OCD

It bothers me

I need to know

Why OCD

ain't CDO

21: Vinyl

There's not much I'm a stickler for

but on this, my view is final

The way to blast your favourite tunes

is certainly on Vinyl

A crackle that makes you feel all warm
The lyrics on the sleeve

Even a jump that feels like home

confirms me to believe

That progress isn't always right
If it ain't broke, don't fix it

You can take your download if you prefer

but I bet that you can't mix it

22: Eating during a headstand

A wise man once said
it's not good to eat bread
whilst stood on you head
so I had soup instead

I must now confess
that I made quite a mess
all over my dress
t'was twad foolish I guess

23: Aristotle

It is not well known but Aristotle
invented the hot water bottle
He delivered them in his ford capri
so there'd be less goosebumps for you and me

If you think I'm fibbing, have a google
He thought it up with his friend, Dougal
You're doubting me, "Ange, don't you shame
us"
but do you really know what made him
famous

I was just joking but now I bet
you're reaching for the internet
for the hot water bottle was made by who
and what did Aristotle do

24: Reach

'Leaf me alone'
said the tree to the squirrel
'I don't want to talk
so please go away Cyril
I don't feel myself
My look is all ragged
so leaf me to cry
for my bark that is sagged'
The squirrel looked sad
at his dear friend, the tree
He responded 'My word,
now you listen to me.
Your leaves are all splendid
in orange and gold
and just cos you've lost some
don't mean that you're old
Sometimes things change
as a new season starts

but we'll always be us
deep down in our hearts
So straighten your trunk
and reach for the sky
It might take a day
or two but please try'
The tree now looked down
at his roots, strong and firm
He felt quite embarrassed
for having a squirm
'Cyril my friend
You really are wise
I'll be proud now and happy
I need no disguise
I'll show my bare branches
until new leaves grow
and I'll still be loved
by the creatures I know'.
I'm happy to share that
the brave tree soon found
his leaves that had fallen

down onto the ground
became memories adorning
his beautiful base
and he reached for the sky
with new joy on his face

25: Sweetcorn

How can we trust food that doesn't digest
It doesn't seem right to me
I gave up on Sweetcorn from when I was 9
until I was 43

Some say I'm foolish
I've heard them mutter
Corn on the cob is
well lush with butter

But I find it quite scary
I think you should too
It looks the same on your plate
as it does in your poo

26: Awakening Spring

Away with the cold, away with the night
The flowers unfold and look up to the light

The unfrozen stream babbles over the ground
Winters gone like a dream as Spring comes
around

Wildlife emerge from their places of slumber
at first in doubt but assured by their number

The Butterflies dance and the Hummingbirds
sing
at the joyous romance of awakening Spring

27: Giraffe Rhymes

There's probably already a poem
about a big tall giraffe
and how long it took to knit
his big long beautiful scarf

But I thought I'd still write this
'cos it made me laugh
but nowt rhymes with giraffe
unless he's in a bath

28: If I won the Lottery

If I won the lottery
I guess I'd feel that I was free
I'd go and dance out in the rain
I'd pack my case and head to Spain

I'd get a tattoo of my ticket
and tell my job where they can stick it
I'd sleep each day until the noon
and never leave the pub too soon

But then I guess that I would miss
my life that's really pretty bliss
I'd miss my loved ones and I'd miss the perk
Of 20% discount at my work

Maybe a compromise, I'll just be
a millionaire when it suits me
so pass the cheque and pop the fizz
in case my boss has just read this

29: I like Cheese

I like Cheese on Crackers
On Jacket potatoes too
On Pasta and on toast
In solid form or goo

I like Cheese on Pizza
and on Naan bread as well
Cheddar, Mozzarella
Dolcelatte, Babybel

I like Cheesy chips
and Crisps and Straws and Pastry
I like Cheese on everything
because it's super tasty

30: The boys who kicked the ball

(my Ode to Reading gaol)

I looked from my office window as boredom
began to call
For a second I felt jealous of the boys who
kicked the ball

Then I looked beyond their goalposts at the
wall that gripped the space
The air they breathed was fresh but outside
ended in that place

Young men who'd made their choices, felt
that they'd been born to fail
and now they kicked a ball about the grounds
of Reading Gaol

I felt less trapped in my office, the clock now ticked less slowly
I could walk around at leisure and never feel that lonely

Then I watched them as they laughed and called to a new mate
That friend that knew them better cos they'd shared this broken fate

I thought maybe I was wrong that their path was at the end
Maybe their path had found the place where they could start to mend

To find kindreds who just got them with no judging and no greed
They ran and played together and I hope it sowed a seed
The walls were just as high no matter what their class

Their clocks would tick the same till another
day could pass

I wonder what became of them, so young
with time ahead
I hope their lives that followed were of freer
times instead

Each time they took a pass or won as a whole
team
I hope it made them proud and I hope it
made them dream

Maybe they kept in touch with the boys who
kicked the ball
now that beyond their goalposts, there's no
longer a wall

31: St Bernards

It's great to be a St Bernard
although some things can be quite hard
To fit through there and squeeze through here
can sometimes cause my Mumma fear

You can't carry me like a Pug
but darn I give the bestest hug
and if you're brave we'll head outside
and I can take you for a ride

32: Pa's on the roof

The day Pa climbed up on the roof we feared
that he would jump
He'd seemed so jolly earlier with no sign of
the hump
He hid beneath the satellite dish and only had
one welly
Then under closer scrutiny we saw he had the
telly

What on earth is going on, my mother
shouted madly
If you want some time alone, I'll leave you to
it gladly
but the tv's getting wet and, god forbid, the
vids
Now get yourself back down here, you're
worrying the kids

Pa peered down and shook his head, he folded
his arms firmly
I'm not coming back down there when you're
looking up so sternly
I can't hear what's going on when you all
make a riot
and now you've all followed me here when I
just want some quiet

Oh Pa, come down, called little Sam, I'm
missing you already
We'll let you listen to your show, I'll be quiet
as teddy
So Pa climbed down and that day marked
the start of something new
Now when Pa watched Robot wars we quietly
watched it too

33: 2020's lessons

2020 was a learning curve
to say the very least
We had to adapt quickly
to slay a nasty beast

Some of us got fitter
Some began to bake
We took on DIY tasks
and we took all we could take

But we learnt that we're resilient
we're tougher than we thought
We had a go at quizzes
and zoom lessons were taught

So what's the biggest lesson
I'll tell you if you ask
Good heavens don't eat marmite
before putting on your mask

34: Maggie and Dom

(A catch up with our dear friends from Here I Go Again)

The year that Maggie went to Ibiza
she strived to leave the ground beneath her

She challenged herself from her comfort zone
but her boyfriend Dom said, "You're on your
own.

Just because I ride a bike,
there's something 'bout heights I just don't
like"

Maggie laughed "Don't be afraid
Being daring's how dreams are made.

Enjoy your morning, I'll be back soon"
and she jumped aboard a hot air balloon

That evening at dinner she gasped with glee.
"I really am so proud of me"

"Me too" said Dom "I don't know how
you'll surpass all you have done now".
Maggie beamed "I have a plan
tomorrow I know just how I can."

Dom smiled inside, because he knew
he'd been a little daring too.

Next day as Maggie neared a helicopter
Dom appeared and gently stopped her

"Well this is crazy but I'm coming too
I want to be everywhere with you."

As they ascended, Dom looked in her eyes
"Maggie, dear. I've a little surprise.

"You've ticked things off your bucket list

and I'm inspired. I couldn't resist."

With that, Dom gave a massive grin
and revealed a beautiful diamond ring.

"Darling Maggie. I thought I'd see
if you would like to marry me."

"Oh yes my love. I defo would
That really sounds so very good."

When they'd landed Maggie saw
her feet now rarely touched the floor

Her soul soared high, tho on the ground
whenever her sweetheart was around

And so it was, the day did come
when our Maggie and Dom became one

They thanked the stars for their daring day
as a helicopter whisked them both away

35: Top five to ten per cent

I did a quiz I found online
I thought that it would pass the time
Well it seemed that it was time well spent
Aa it said I'm in the top percent

To move round shapes was just one task
The memory stuff was a bit of an ask
I thought oh no I've failed, but then
It said I was the top five to ten

I jumped for joy, I cried a bit
Oh wow I'm clever, not just fit
and then I made the dreadful error
of giving this info to my fella

Now each time I say something daft
before he simply would have laughed
but it seems his memory is heaven sent
As he lols "top five to ten percent"

36: Pink Flamingos

Roses are red
Flamingos are pink....

but they weren't always
They became pink from eating algae
that contained carotenoid pigments
The same can be said of shrimp
but not of Alecia Moore, the singer
She decided to become p!nk but did
not eat carotenoided algae in order to do so

37: Hay Fever

I love Flowers
I love Bees
but god damn pollen
makes me sneeze

Can't be awake
without a tissue
Every year
the same old issue

The reddened eyes
of damn hay fever
making me look
like a diva

Took a pill
cos I felt lousy
I'm still snotty but
nice and drowsy

38: Reflection of a Buttercup

The perfect beauty of a child's joy
at the simplest of things
The skimming of a pebble
creating magic rings

A ladybird comes visiting
and causes wonderous awe
New visions grace their every day
and sounds not heard before

The reflection of a Buttercup
held beneath a tilted chin
lighting up a tiny face
with a quite delighted grin

Each moment an adventure
such treasures to behold
Be grateful if they invite you
to share these times of gold

39: Lived to Tell

I feel so lucky to be here
We've experienced another year
We've lived, we've loved and how we've
laughed
We've learnt some things and acted daft

Let's take a moment to remember
The joys from January to December
The known, the new, the big surprises
The tumbles followed by the rises

I'd like to thank with all of my heart
each one of you that played a part
The big occasion, the captured minute
What a year! Glad I was in it!

40: I'd like to be your Tubigrip

I'd like to be your tubigrip
so I can fix your pain
I'd squeeze you nice and tightly
til you feel good again

I'd manipulate your tendons
so they're where they're s'posed to be
and make no bones about it
that you should be held by me

41: On the buses

I never thought I'd make a fuss
'bout journeying upon the bus
After many months of covid fever
I really am an eager beaver

I'm ready with my cleaning gel
my gloves are packed, my mask as well
I'm like a kid who gets the treat
of sitting tall on their own seat

I'll say good morning to the driver
And thank the Lord I'm a survivor
I'll relish every sight and sound as
the wheels on the bus go round and round

I hope by time this rhyme is read
Bus fear's a memory in our head
but I hope we remember and refer
to how brave all our bus drivers were

42: A growing Dinosaur

Once there was a Dinosaur
He liked to stomp. He liked to roar
He loved Ice cream upon the beach
and the juiciest leaves only Daddy could reach

"Mummy Mummy." He would call her
"When, oh when will I be taller"
"If you eat your food my dear, you'll see
You grow as big as your Daddy"

One day his Father called from high
"Come up here Son, look at this sky"
Our Dino took a breath and tried
As Daddy watched his pup with pride

He reached his head above the trees
as Mammoths passed by at his knees
He ate the top leaves with his Dad
and laughed with joy. "Wow, this is mad."

"Mama was right, she told me so
Mum's really are the ones who know
Oh Dad, Hurray, at last it's true
I really am as tall as you".

43: Superfoods

Sleep had been flaky
It appeared that we'd rowed
I'd just woken yet needed a nap
So I headed for sugar
in fruit, you're allowed
and a Blueberry rolled in my lap

I thought is that a sign
as it bounced off my phone
and rolled down my t-shirt with glee
to cancel all plans
maybe stay at home
even superfoods were out to get me

Then that made me laugh
as I thought of wee capes
wrapped round every sweet Blueberry
Each heroic morsel
getting into scrapes

but now they were coming for me
Now stop it I thought
you're just a bit tired
It's time now to get up and go
I smiled and went out
as the carpet was mired
by a Blueberry stuck to my toe

The moral of this story
is nothing I fear
This tip just may take you far though
Beware the superfoods
the threat there is clear
so be dressed when you eat Avocado

44: Big bouncy Elastic band ball

I wondered today about something absurd
Pray tell if you've wondered at all
Is there a record, has anyone heard
For a big bouncy elastic band ball

Mine is now really something to behold
You never quite know when you'll need it
However it seems that I don't take bands off
Just seem to continue to feed it

Could there be rules 'bout how big it should
get
and where would you ever dispose it
I'm rather confuddled so ping me a line
if anyone actually knows it

45: Puddles

When rainy days come
and life is a muddle
you're never too old
to splash in a puddle

So pull on your wellies
yes right now, make haste
and go get-a-stomping
Dry boots are a waste

Don't be put off if
bystanders look wary
It's only because they
think puddles are scary

Just tell them it's swell
and to give it a bash
You might brighten their day
when they too have a splash

46: What now cometh after

The fog is lifting
and dreams are drifting
back into our hearts

After the knock
we'll now take stock
of whereabouts we are

Hands will be took
those hands that shook
in worry at the start

Loved ones held tight
with all our might
for time we've been apart

Dates will be set
New lovers met
The sound of joyous laughter

At last it seems
it's time for dreams
of what now cometh after

47: Fisticuffs

I was walking through the park one day
when I came across a sight
Ron Burgundy and Macho man
were embroiled in a word fight

I paid to view and headed their way
just in time to hear Macho man say

"I'll elbow drop you man, oooh yeah'
You're crying cos I've better hair"
Waving his flute, Ron shouted "darn it,
I spent two hours on this barnet."

Macho man glared at him and could
agree his newsreader hair was good
but better than his? he'd be amazed
His slick response left burgundy dazed

"I'm too hot to handle and too cold to hold"

Now our Ron's on the ropes, surely he'd fold

Then came a low blow, "your leotard's grassy"

Ron finished him off with a "You stay classy"

Macho man said "I'm cream of the crop

but fair play man, you're also quite top"

Ron shook his hand "you can join my news team".

This story shows we can all live our dream

48: This is just what happens now

What day is it I ask once more
while I reheat my coffee
and darn it, I forgot that I need bread

Where have I just put my spoon
I swear that I just had it
If it weren't screwed on I swear I'd lose my head

Drink re-warmed, I sit to watch
that programme thingy's in
cos whatsisname has told me that it's good

I've a niggle I've forgot something
but I can't remember what
and I'd only recall it briefly if I could

So this is just what happens now
Each task is an adventure
I can never say that any day's a bore

I'd write it on a post it note
somewhere safe I guess
but I've forgotten what I got my pen out for

49: Stuck in the bath

I remember the day
It was such a laugh
when we realised Aunt Sal
had got stuck in the bath

A mishap with her toe
whilst trying to wash it
caused her to become
at one with the fossett

When the firemen came
we threw her a throw
and they freed Aunt Sal
from her embarrassed woe

The strange things they'd seen
and where they'd been stuck
made our Aunt Sal's toe
seem just slightly bad luck

Aunt Sal was released
in just under an hour
and from that day forward
she opted to shower

50: Parping

There's no set age to stop your giggles
when out of your bottom, a blow off wiggles

Parping's awesome, we all must face it
Best thing to do is just embrace it

Even grown-ups sometimes laugh
when they make bubbles in the bath

Mum might complain because they smell
but we all know she parps as well

Not everything this fun is free
so next time that you have a wee

don't even try to get a grip
Just seize the day and let one rip

51: Healing light

I was feeling wide awake
so put a meditation on
Three rings of the chimes
and my eyes had nearly gone

I sank into the mattress
as the nice man told me to
Imagined I was in the sea
all sparkly and new

I took my special breaths
I cleared my head of thinking
consumed amongst the waves now
I'm sinking and I'm sinking

I'm tingly as I follow
an imaginary light
moving slowly through my body
making everything feel right

Then a message on my phone
interrupts before it's done
now I'm all calm and sleepy
but a light shines out my bum

52: Magpie

Oh you naughty magpie
I thought you were my mate
If I saw you alone
we'd sit together and we'd wait

I'd say 'where's your buddy'
and it often wasn't long
till your love would come to join you
in your quite distinctive song

Then one day I watched you
you searched for bugs with greed
You seemed a bit distracted
concentrating on your feed

You didn't see me salute
or tell your buddies what you'd found
You busily kept on pulling
all the worms out of the ground

It bothered me a little
that you didn't look my way
I only realise now you had
a warning for my day
Eventually your friends came down
and then a few of mine
but I guess I should have noticed
when you gave your sorrow sign

Later that day it happened
my buddy left my side
I guess that time had beaten us
but we enjoyed the ride

So now I'm on my lonesome
but I have a pretty hew
I'm bigger than the cute birds
and my wings are floppy too

but I've found I have the chat

just like you and I am bold
and I possess such treasure
my loved ones are pure gold

So next time please say Hi
don't feel mournful for my sorrow
We'll still be buddies magpie
and salute a brighter morrow

53: A new blank cassette

As I grow older I'll never forget
the absolute joy of a new blank cassette
Endless excitement of what to record
creative hours and memories stored

Taping the charts on a Sunday night
pressing the button just at the right
moment as the talking stops
counting down what's top of the pops

Writing the labels as neat as could be
listening hard as you couldn't see
google to check who sang that song
Leaving a gap in case you guess wrong

Checking newspapers to fill in the spaces
then colour coding all of the cases
labelled and dated like treasure displayed
the proud exhibition of each cassette made

Now if you're lucky you just might still own
a few of those tapes, a reminder of home
or hear in your head a song finish then start
the next one that followed back then in the
chart

I often wonder as I press play
how many others were taping that day
how many still own the very same list
of songs written neatly with some artists
missed

Creative hours and memories stored
endless excitement of what to record
The absolute joy of a new blank cassette
As I grow older I'll never forget

54: Are we there yet?

Are we there yet, I asked once more
Not yet, the driver replied
But I want to get there now I said
The driver looked and sighed

But once you're there, what then my dear
He paused for my next gripe
I didn't really know, I said
He parked and filled his pipe

We're halfway there, now stop and look
I followed his pointed finger
Look here, right now, at where you are
Are you sure that you won't linger?

In my haste to rush the journey
to my next destination
I needed this, to notice now
this day and it's elation

55: Farewell to my eyebrow

There are some things we're prepared for
as age creeps up upon
our poor old sorry arses
but darn it this is wrong

One day I woke quite different
a brand new wrinkle came
a bloody thing so prominent
I'd swear it had a name

It weren't just it's arrival
the fact that it was there
but the feature that it had replaced
my dear old eyebrow hair

This crater went right through it
like an earthquake on the ground
the other eyebrow was just fine
I searched and quickly found

So I didn't just discover
that I was no longer thatched
the situation's worse cos
my eyebrows are mismatched

So farewell to my eyebrow
I only wish I knew
Did you come out or go back in
just where the hell are you

Farewell to my eyebrow
a pencil has been bought
I thought I knew it all but
some things are just not taught

56: Muffins for the Puffins

Did you hear 'bout the Puffins
who liked eating Muffins
although they would leave lots of crumbs

They would try to tidy
each week on a Friday
till they realised they didn't have thumbs

This made it so tricky
their eating got picky
and they only ate now when fed

But of this, they got bored
Muffins were restored
and they hired a cleaner instead

57: A drink or ten

There was a lady lived near me
who liked Prosecco with her tea
A little Gin at breakfast time
and with her lunch, a glass of Wine

One day the Doctor came a calling
"You're middle aged. This is appalling"
The lady laughed and slammed Tequila
"But Sir it's a well-known ancient healer"

The Doctor said "how do you feel?
You shouldn't drink all this for real"
She laughed at him, it had her tickled
"Dear boy, I'm fine. I'm nicely pickled"

The Doctor cleared his throat and said
"I worry soon you may be dead"
"Do stop", she laughed "I can't take more
You fool, I'm bloomin' ninety four"

58: Purple

Nothing rhymes with purple
It really is a shame
It's such a lovely colour
with such an obscure name

I tried to write a poem
To share that I'm a fan
but I can't do no rhyming
so I'm not sure that I can

59: Use it or lose it

They say use it or lose it
but I couldn't guess
that that would relate
to my drinking prowess

I thought I'd get healthy
so had a small break
but I didn't foresee
what a change it would make

Now I'm a lightweight
I'm drunk on a sniff
and that's just Prosecco
that's not even stiff

Imagine a Whiskey
I might go doolally
Before when I drank
I'd just get real pally

But now I'm a nuisance
although safe at home
I'm repeating myself
and jeez, please hide my phone
and Oh man, the hangover
now I'm a food slut
not sure I'll survive
without help from The Hut

But the thought of teetotalling
makes me feel heady
I know that it's wise
but I'm not sure I'm ready

Maybe I'll practise
one sip at a time
Maybe not start
with three bottles of Wine

Maybe stop when i'm tipsy

and stay off the Rum
and leave parties before I've
fell down on my bum

I guess watch this space
and I will try lots
to sensibly drink
unless someone says Shots

60: I'd like to be a Penguin

I'd like to be a Penguin
I like the way they waddle
I'd walk around all day
and talk a load of twaddle

Whenever I was chilly
I would just give a shrug
and waddle to my buddies
to have a little hug

61: Kicking off

I've woken up with Butterflies
and I'll tell you the reason
After waiting all the summer long
It's first day of the season

The slate's wiped clean
The table's clear
We wonder
will this be our year?

of record wins
run in the cup
all chanting
We are going up

It's kick off time
where are we heading
To the Mad Stad
Come on Reading!

62: Leaky Pen

I seem to have a leaky pen
It's ink is on my hand
but I can't see where it's coming from
I just don't understand

The pen looks absolutely fine
and mostly writes ok
but every now and then it seems
the ink just gets away

I can't tell when it will occur
so I'll hold a little tighter
onto my pen and let it know
it's a very special writer

Sometimes chapters go awry
or words don't come out right
but I 've let my little pen know now
it's not a solo fight

Many a good pen sometimes leaks
although it looks ok
but I shall give it time and love
It shan't be thrown away

63: Sunrise

The little flower stirred it's leaves
and peeped out from it's petals
it appeared it was the starting of the morn

He hid away for one more moment
wondering was it time
the sleepy flower gave a little yawn

He peeped again and saw a shadow
creep across the soil
teasing him to come on out to play

and as he fought away his slumber
he knew that it was time as
a blackbird sang it's greeting to the day

The little flower stretched his fronds
and unfolded gracefully as his
neighbours also woke throughout the bed

and in perfect time the little flower
stood up proud and tall
to greet the new sunrise upon his head

64: My Pagoda

I once had a Pagoda
to erect it took some labour
so imagine my dismay
when it flew over to my neighbour

I tried another briefly
I thought it would be trusty
but again the bugger blew away
as soon as it was gusty

So now I'm on my 3rd
it's big and bright and red
If I lose this one I'm giving up
and sitting in the shed

65: The Flamencoing Flamingo

Up in Space the Flamingo views
The planet Earth all over the news
Sadness spread from Jamaica to France
as people forgot how to dance

As smiles faded, they couldn't think
just what was the missing link
to bring back joy into their lives
they must teach Ballet to under fives

Tap in Kitchens was a must
Acrobatics in the dust
A little Tango would bring a grin
To have forgotten was a sin

From the dark, there came a light
"Hello my friends, It'll be alright
I'm here to save the human race

I'm a Flamencoing Flamingo from outer
Space''

Steps were taught and laughs were heard
Such happiness from just one bird
The humans vowed to take a stance
to never again forget to dance

66: I'm not a Cat

We'd been locked down a long time now
thought things couldn't get much stranger
despite our distance we all felt close
as we hid from the same danger

Little things, they became huge
as we looked online for fun
Grandmas learnt what Tik tok was
and Jay's quiz was number one

Just as we became accustomed
and thought that that was that
just one man got us all stating
that we were not a cat

and people waited with baited breath
for a parish council's zoom
We shouted 'read the standing orders'
like we were in the room

I hope that when this storm has passed
the thing we'll keep forever
is the interest in the little things
that kept us all together

67: There's something you should know

There's something you should know my friend
said the badger to the bear
I guess you think it's secret
but they know you poo in there

68: Rugby nerves

What's wrong with your fella
he's looking quite yella
I'm worried about the poor bugger
I saw basically
he looks panicky
whenever he watches the rugger

Don't worry, he's fine
This dear man of mine
but occasions can get to him greatly
The build up is loud
with the songs from the crowd
and there's been loads of rule changes lately

I too am a fan
and I know the nerves can
sometimes make you feel a bit icky
Knock ons and rule changes
Turnovers, long ranges

makes being a fan a bit tricky
There's one small thing though
that I just can't let go
It's making me worry you see
We'll grip our seats tight
pray with all our might
but your fella's the match referee

69: Tequila

One Tequila, two Tequila, three Tequila, four
I was fine a mo ago but now it seems I'm on
the floor

I may have paid the price for swinging on my
chair
Now my head is in the bin and my legs are in
the air

I worked hard all week long so I had a little
drink
Next I was singing Let it go whilst sitting in
the sink

The only saving grace is that I'm safely in my
room
but the mortifying thing is that my friends
are here on zoom

70: Political posts

It's hard not to post about politics
when our country's run by a bunch of dicks

Every day there's another story
of an epic fail by some dumb Tory

Please believe, I don't like fighting
I do hold back sometimes from writing

but of frustrations I have a wealth
so if i've posted, it's for my health

71: The Elephant and Parrot

When the Elephant met the Parrot
he could not believe his ears
as his words were echoed back to him
he laughed himself to tears

A bird who said it enjoyed mud
and had a big long trunk
and a very rounded bottom
well, Elie felt like he was drunk

The Parrot was a little miffed
he was only repeating
It was his special talent
so why was our Elie bleating?

He thought he'd play a little trick
so when the elephant spoke
instead of echoing his sound
the Parrot gave a croak

"Oh no, a Frog" our Elephant squealed
The Parrot laughed with glee
"Ha ha" said Parrot and confused him more
"That croaking came from me"

"You what?" said Elie. "Now I'm stumped
What sound is really yours?"
"Well everything" responded Parrot
"from Mice to slamming doors".

"Well well" said Elie. "I'll have a bet
there's one sound you can't do"
He pulled out an old tape cassette
labelled Rush's Xanadu

Elie was right, he won that day
because he'd tried already
The Parrot might be awesome
but no-one can echo Geddy

72: Don't leave completely

I thought I'd never sing again
Now I love my radio
Thought my dancing days were over
but I'm swaying to and fro

My laughter left me for a while
but that just isn't me
I like to lose my senses till
I'm running for a wee

I thought my world had ended
with you not here to complete me
I'm winning one day at a time
but please don't leave completely

73: One for the road

I'm young at heart and feeling fit
but this truth hurts, it's such a git

that one for the road now seems to be
not one more drink but one more wee

74: Treatwalking

It seems I've developed quite a knack
of sleeping through my midnight snack

There's wrappers here under the covers
of Wotsits, Quavers and some others

Nuts and sweet bags on the floor
Seems I need calories to snore

Also appears I can unwrap
a Chocolate bar during my nap

I didn't get the whole bar in
as there's still smudges on my chin

and what is this upon my knees
How on earth did I grate cheese

If there's food it seems I'll grab it
I've invented a new habit

75: Firework

He wowed her like a firework
but it transpired he was a berk
It took a little time to clock it
but then she gave that guy a rocket

With his misdemeanours now amounting
and his tankard missing from The Fountain
she caught him at the Catherine wheel
sharing sparklers with Lucille

His apologies were oft and many
but she didn't give that guy a penny
She kept her spark and he soon learnt
that too much banging gets you burnt

76: My own advice

Drink water with your alcohol
and line your tummy first
Booze on an empty stomach
makes hangovers their worst

Wouldn't it be nice
if I took my own advice

You can quit the ciggies
You'll soon be feeling great
Have an ice pop when you're craving
It'll pass, you just must wait

Wouldn't it be nice
if I took my own advice

Exercise when you're cranky
Pizza's not the answer
Get fresh air and wiggle

God's special tiny dancer
Wouldn't it be nice
if I took my own advice

Save money for a rainy day
The whole pub don't need your drinks
A sad bank statement exacerbates
a hangover that stinks

Wouldn't it be nice
if I took my own advice

Make good changes to your life
Growth deserves your time,
stamina and dedication
Please don't just write a rhyme

Wouldn't it be nice
if I took my own advice

77: The grinning things

It's a gift that when one's feeling down
there's joy to lift both heart and frown
by those that don't yet know the bad
one smile from them can fight the sad

The young to whom we give our care
who also heal us when we're there
a twinkling eye, a hug that sings
we're rescued by the grinning things

The glow of unconditional love
a heart that's never had enough
of you and every quirk and trait
Those are the bits they think are great

The music as they say your name
and ask when you'll come play again
fresh strength to handle all life brings
once rescued by the grinning things

78: Sprouts

As I write about food
there's one I've left out
controversially famous
the old brussel sprout

Some people adore them
and worry of frost
or of overcooking
causing taste to be lost

Some have just one
on their Christmas plate
as a sign of respect
on this one special date

Others are passionate
they're close to their heart
they don't mind the smell
of the next morning's fart

It's a splendid debate
that never will end
is the Brussel a foe
or a green tasty friend

79: Making Dolphins

I surprised myself by getting a buzz
from playing Badminton with my cuz
It made us happy, we deduced
as apparently dolphins are produced

We ran around and waved our bats
we'd feared that we would look like prats
Yet I'm glad to say we're pretty flair
at keeping our cocks in the air

We ensured to replenish fluids spent
It is instructed, I'm sure they meant
that for each session of our sporting career
we should then go out and drink some beer

80: Real Housewives of Woodley

I love the Real housewives
Big fan of them all
I cheer their successes
and cringe when they fall

To decide on a favourite
is tricky I fear
but I'd love to binge watch
The Real housewives of here

Real housewives of Woodley
Oh we'd make a show
Think how many funny
Woodley gals you know

So Andy Cohen
I think that we'd fit
Give us a shot and
we'll give you a hit

81: Acceptance of denial

It's beer o'clock we like to say
but don't give it a time
As long as midday's hit somewhere
we concur that it is fine

The sun is here so we need to be
out tanning with our G&T
then next day we feel like shits
we're feeling sick and burnt our tits

But how can it be bad
when it's just made from a berry
It makes us want to dance and sing
and do stuff which is merry

We drink too much. Probs should stop
It makes me want to blub
We'll have a chat about it
when I see you down the pub

82: I'd like to be your flannel

I'd like to be your flannel
so I can touch your face
I'd rub along your body
at my own delighted pace

I'd slowly rub your shoulders
then pat you on the bum
I'd do it so you're nice and clean
then once again for fun

83: Who's playing Bass

Don't fret said the guitar
as the drum kept banging on
We'll listen to the bass
and we'll just play along

The tambourine looked at the bass
Do you know what's coming now
I don't but the guitar will know
He played with Holy Cow

The guitar headed to the drums
Are we counting in on four?
I've no idea mate what we're playing
now that they want more

The mic stand did a headstand
to pass the time of day
Ok Wembley it's up to you
now tell us what to play

The instruments all sighed, relieved
now that they had a plan
till just one joker shouted out
Play one that you can

The drums decided on a 13/8
That made the others shiver
Oh damn they shouted, now we're screwed
He's sold us down the river

But as we're here we'll have a go
Come on guys let's try it
so they done it and they done it good
and it went down a riot

84: Champagne and Celery

I went to see if I had an allergy
To be as healthy as I could be
My age was that it now would matter
if my tummy was happy and slightly flatter

Well first the Dairy had to go
Cow's milk's not for humans, don't ya know
Ok, there's substitutes for that
I'll cry about Cheese but it made me fat

I need a break from foods like Toms
so no more greenhouse delights from Mom's
Then came Potatoes and even Yeast
there goes Chips and my Marmite
feasts

Then came the words, no Wheat or Gluten
Now I'm upset and I'm disputing
No Bread, no Pizza what hell is this

What will I eat when I'm on the piss

Then came a lifeline, if I obey, and try it
I can bring some things back into my diet
So yes that really is what you see
I'm living on Champagne and Celery

85: When Elon meets the Martians

I'd like to be a fly
upon the wall one day
when Elon meets the Martians
I wonder what they'll say

I dreamt once they admired
his objective to roam
It seemed that he'd been there before
as he was welcomed home

Maybe he's their leader
and there'll be lots of clapping
but maybe he was banished
and they will swiftly zap him

Maybe this won't happen
the odds are pretty steep
Maybe I should stop
eating cheese before I sleep

86: Words

I sometimes feel the words I write
have all been said before
I'm not sure if I have new thoughts
of my own anymore
I take in all encouragement
from songs and social pages
then when I want to write myself
it takes me bloomin' ages
There's only so many words you see
and phrases I could use
to get my point across to you
To help escape the blues
So Express yourself, we're halfway there
and don't you stop believing
Get the party started, Twist and shout
and go dancing on the ceiling
Oops, here comes the copyright charges
hope I don't get put away
If so I pray that at least these words
have made you have a smile today

87: Dolly's remedy

I felt the tide was pulling
didn't even dare to dream
that we could stay afloat
and find an island in the stream

Dolly parton had enough
and she showed her love was true
so now we join to say
Dolly, we'll always love you

Jolene, it made some money
and now Dolly had a plan
she helped out with a vaccine
so this shit won't take my man

now I'm not crying 9 to 5
and I finally feel free
I've had a shot into my arm
of Dolly's remedy

88: Nature's Joy

The twinkle of frost upon a leaf
catches my eye and I look up from my path
The road ahead fades for a brief moment
as this beauty fills my heart with joy

Sweet nature surrounds me just as the birds
do tell
I thank the trees for waving me on my
journey
along the path
which now appears less daunting

89: Nose Hair

There's nothing like a nose hair
for ruining your day
The perfect confirmation
that time has had it's way

When one is young and free
with hair flying in the breeze
you don't anticipate that
just after a sneeze

The only hair that's flying
is the nasal dweller now
I guess it's there to balance out
the demise of one's eyebrow

90: I wandered slowly as a cloud

I wandered slowly as a cloud
that lingers on the Sun
It starts quite small then sits there proud
you probably know the one

The jeopardiser of one's tan
we will to move away
As right now I have no plan
I'm slow as that today

91: Pup-ular

Whilst chilling one day
A friend turned to say
that he'd wanted a way
to paint dogs if they'd stay

I'd like them to dine
on food that is fine
I think a Canine
could have taste just like mine

What a pup..ular hit
he added with wit
if they all would just sit
quite still for a bit

Imagine his mood
A satisfied dude
All they needed was food
and the dogs posed and chewed

A large pack of Poodles
now sat eating Noodles
which they enjoyed oodles
and he got his doodles

92: Butterflies

The dancing white butterflies
remind us you're there
still watching us closely
we're still in your care

93: Grandad

My Grandad set the bar real high
To be our best and always try

He sang, he danced and told great jokes
I see his wit in all my folks

Offered more tea, he'd make me laugh
when responding each time, "I'll 'ave 'alf'

A man so sweet and yet so brave
He inspired us all how to behave

When we talk of him we thank the
stars
We are so blessed that he was ours

94: Twinkle twinkle

Twinkle twinkle little blim
Will you ever fade to dim
Burning through the carpet tile
like an inch that spreads a mile
Twinkle twinkle little blim
Will you ever fade to dim

95: Captain Tom

One day in 1920
a baby boy was born
I expect his parents never had a clue
that everyone would know his name
before his final dawn
cos of everything he did for me and you

At 99 he woke one day
and got his trainers out
and walked and walked while we were
drinking Gin
he made us smile and gave us hope
inspiration replaced doubt
we'd try each day to be a bit like him

He hoped to raise a thousand pounds
to help the Nhs
and once we heard, the funds began to soar
when he hit a million

I bet he wouldn't guess
that there'd be nearly 40 million more
The more we learned, the more we loved
he'd been a hero way back when
like many, he had served, no hesitation
I wonder how the troops would cheer
if they had known back then
he'd be number one on every music station

He taught us not to waste a day
and never doubt our worth
each one of us could really make a mark
He punched the air with happiness
and shared with us his mirth
he charmed us with his enigmatic spark

His 100th birthday came along with
150,000 cards
thanks sent by every person they were from
a flypast and a knighthood
and the nation's best regards
to the wee boy who became our Captain Tom

96: The Green Tractor

I followed a green tractor
It really made my day
It was all big and shiny
and all covered with hay
I followed the green tractor
to go and see it's farm
I'll just see if there are others
It can't do any harm
The Farmer, he thought different
"Stop bothering my sheep
I'll go and get my rifle
if you keep being a creep"
"But I really like green tractors"
I had to quickly say
"I just wanted to see it's home
Now I'll be on my way"
"You'll earn your keep now first boy"
He pointed to the wheat
So I got to drive the tractor
and my day was really neat

97: Mirror mirror

Mirror mirror on the wall
Why've you made my eyelids fall
and my bits I thought were perky
are reflected like a Christmas Turkey

That there wrinkle just can't be
when in my head, I'm twenty three
What you're showing can't be true
You're a bugger, We are through

98: When having a shower is effort

I should get up and have a shower
Been thinking it for o'er an hour

I'm sitting here and really wishing
it didn't seem like such a mission

I'll have some energy you see
once the shower invigorates me

but I need a shower first to glean
the energy to then get clean

Once I feel the water trickle
I'll wonder why I'm in a pickle

Then I'll be so glad with me
I'm getting up on one...two...three

ooh a notification on Facebook
might be important, better look..

99: Be ok Tomorrow

Today had been a grotty day
both the weather and my woes
so I snuggled on the sofa
and I covered me in throws

I reached out for the chocolate
and my tv choice was bad
I continued watching utter pants
until I lost my sad

I watched a little comedy
and soon it made me giggle
I listened to some cheesy tunes
and had a little wiggle

I'll be ok tomorrow
and better for today
cos nothing beats a dose of daft
to chase the blues away

100: Age

It's always been a puzzle to me
how when we're young we long to be
Taller, wider, stronger, bolder
We just can't wait until we're older

Yet once we're there we all look back
to when life was easy, slower, a crack
We then discover a new hunger
and we wish now that we were younger

But at last there comes an age of peace
when you can wrap up snug under a fleece
whilst drinking shots and being crazy
You can be wild but still be lazy

So never fear, that day does come
when all is good and all wishing's done
You'll wake up and be pleased to see
you're just the age you want to be

101: Reviews

If you like what I've written
please add a review
cos then I just might
sell another book too

And then there's my ego
so if you're a mate
Use poetic licence
And please tell me I'm great

Printed in Great Britain
by Amazon

10007129R10088